THE ABBOT

As told by Josie the Cat

by Sarah Elizabeth Cowie • illustrated by Sarah Selby

CONCILIAR PRESS
Ben Lomond, California

The Abbot and I:
As told by Josie the Cat

Published by Conciliar Press
P.O. Box 76
Ben Lomond, California 95005

Printed in Romania

ISBN 1-888212-25-X

Lovingly dedicated to
Father Joseph Langdon
Memory Eternal!

The abbot and I
live in a monastery.

In the morning,
the monks get up very early.
They go to church to pray.
While Batiushka is gone,
I stay at home.

I like to lie
in the sunshine.
When he returns,
we have our morning
meal together.

Then we work.

Everyone in the
monastery works.

Some cook . . .

some garden. . .

some sew. . .

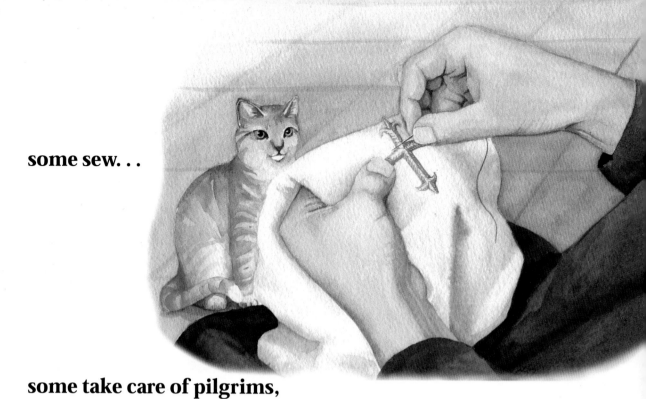

some take care of pilgrims,
some print books.

One of my jobs
is to catch mice.

There is much to be done
in a monastery.
We all love Jesus
very much here,
and do everything for Him.

My abbot's job is to teach the novices
and be a spiritual father.
My job is to help him.
We receive novices and monks in our cell.

We receive pilgrims and nuns in the guest house.
When people come to see us, they knock at the door, saying,
"Lord Jesus Christ, Son of God, have mercy on me a sinner."
My abbot says, "Amen." They come in with a low bow
and go to receive Batiushka's blessing.

Then they come
to greet me.

They sit down and we talk.

Batiushka offers them tea, of course.

I have a treat, if I care to.

I sit in a sunny spot,

and watch all that goes on.

My abbot talks to people

about the love of God

and keeping His commandments.

Some of them have questions or problems.

We help them all we can.

Teaching people and praying for them

is a big part of our job.

Sometimes people want
my abbot to hear their confession.
Batiushka puts on his
epitrachelion and cuffs
and they go into the church.

I stay behind and keep
the abbot's seat warm for him.

When we are alone
in our cell,
Batiushka reads,
takes care of his mail,
or prays.

We are both old.
When we are tired,
we take catnaps.
He naps in his chair,
I nap in the sunshine.

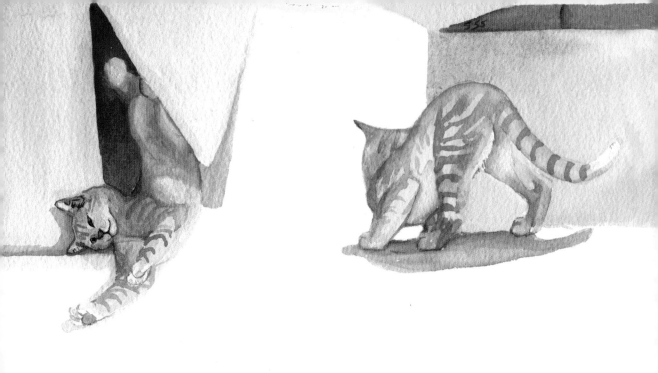

I like to play in boxes, too.

There are a great number
of outdoor cats that live nearby.
We feed them all, every day.
I approve of this almsgiving to the poor.
I watch from the windowsill as they eat.

In the evening, the monks return
to the church for Vespers and Compline.
Afterward, we keep silence.
Before bedtime, there are private
prayers in one's cell and spiritual reading.

On Saturday nights and the eve of feast days,
there is an All-Night Vigil in the church.
Batiushka can be gone a very long time.
This is all right with me.
We all have our own ways of
serving and praising God.
The abbot can't catch mice or purr, after all.

There is a women's monastery nearby.
The abbess and her nuns often come
for these Vigils and Divine Liturgy.

Sundays and feast days are great occasions.
Many pilgrims as well as the nuns come
to the monastery to celebrate the feast. Everyone is joyful.

At church, my abbot will celebrate
the Divine Liturgy with the other clergy.

Afterward, there is a meal for everyone.

On these days, many of the nuns
and pilgrims visit with my abbot.
Sundays and feast days are our biggest
days for visitors. Sometimes we are busy
until evening, when it is time for Vespers.

There are many places a cat could live.

I believe there is no finer place to live than in a monastery.

It's a very noble and blessed life.

We are thankful, the abbot and I.